This
MOUSE WORKS
Classics Collection Storybook

belongs to

Taylor

DISNEY'S
Peter Pan

CLASSIC STORYBOOK

MOUSE WORKS

Find us at **www.disneybooks.com** *for more Mouse Works fun!*

© 1989, 1993, 1997 Disney Enterprises, Inc.
Adapted by Jamie Simons
Illustrated by Atelier Philippe Harchy
Printed in the United States of America
ISBN: 1-57082-801-6
1 3 5 7 9 10 8 6 4 2

CSRVPP97-09

There once was a house in London where a family named
Darling lived. There were Mr. and Mrs. Darling and their three
children, Wendy, John, and Michael. Watching over the children
was Nana, the nursemaid, who also happened to be a dog. It
was to this home that a most interesting visitor came on one
magical starry night. His name was Peter Pan.

Peter Pan chose this house for one very special reason: There were people there who believed in him. Not Mr. Darling. He only thought about business and the importance of being on time and dressing properly. But Mrs. Darling was still young enough at heart to believe that Peter Pan was the spirit of youth.

Then there were John and Michael.
They knew how to fight off pirates,
whoop like Indians, and march like
soldiers. To them Peter Pan was
certainly real, and they made him the
hero of all their games.

8

But the expert on Peter Pan was Wendy. She knew everything there was to know about him.

On this particular night, after Michael and John had drawn a pirate map on their father's shirt front, Mr. Darling angrily declared, "Children need to grow up." Then, turning to Wendy, he added, "This is your last night in the nursery, young lady."

"And there will be no more dogs for nursemaids in this house," Mr. Darling concluded as he marched Nana outside, where he tied her up for the night.

That's how it came to be that when Mr. and Mrs. Darling went out to a party later that night, Wendy, Michael, and John were left all alone, asleep in their room.

A certain boy and his pixie, Tinker Bell, took advantage of the moment and slipped in through the nursery window.

The Darlings' nursery was a familiar place to Peter. He liked to sit in the shadows and listen to Wendy's stories. The hero of these stories was always Peter Pan, of course. But on his last visit, Peter had gotten separated from his shadow. Tonight he had come to get it back.

"Well done, Tink, you've found it!" Peter crowed when Tinker Bell discovered his shadow. But the shadow was in no hurry to be following Peter again. The moment he opened the drawer where it was hiding, the shadow took off, flitting and skittering around the room! Peter charged after it, making such a racket that Wendy woke up!

"Peter Pan! I knew you'd come!" Wendy cried. Then she ran to get her sewing basket. "I saved your shadow for you. It needs sewing on. That's the proper way to do it.

"Oh, Peter, I'm so glad you came back tonight, because it's my last night in the nursery," she added.

16

"But that means no more stories!" cried Peter. "I won't have it! Come on! We're going to Never Land. You'll never grow up there!"

"John! Michael! Wake up...Peter's taking us to Never Land!" cried Wendy. "But Peter, how do we get there?"

"Fly, of course. It's easy. All you have to do is think a wonderful thought. And," said Peter, shaking Tinker Bell, "add a little bit of pixie dust."

"We can fly!" shouted Wendy, John, and Michael as they followed Peter and Tink out the nursery window. They soared over the rooftops of London and past the great clock tower of Big Ben. Peter laughed with glee as he pointed up into the sky.

"There it is, Wendy—Never Land...second star to the right and straight on till morning."

From high up in the sky, they finally spotted the land of their dreams.

"Look, John," cried Wendy, "Mermaid Lagoon!"

"And the Indian Camp!" yelled John.

"There's the pirate ship and its crew," added Michael, all twinkly with excitement. "It's just as you told us, Wendy!"

"Oh, Peter! It's just as I've always dreamed it would be," Wendy smiled.

23

The captain of the pirate ship was a nasty fellow named Hook. He had only one dream in life—to destroy Peter Pan. "Blast that Peter Pan!" said Hook as he studied a map of Never Land. "If I could only find his hideout, I'd trap him."

Captain Hook got his name because he had a hook where a hand should be. And who was to blame for that? Why, Peter Pan, of course. Hook had another enemy, too—the crocodile. He was terrified of the creature. "He's been following me around for years, licking his chops," said Hook.

"And he'd have had you by now, Cap'n, if he hadn't swallowed that alarm clock. Now when he's about, he warns you with his tick-tock, tick-tock…" said Smee.

"Peter Pan, ahoy!" cried the lookout. Instantly Captain Hook forgot about the crocodile. "Swoggle me eyes," he cried, looking through his telescope. "It is Pan!" Ordering his men to load the cannon, Hook fired away!

"Quick, Tink!" shouted Peter as the cannonballs flew by. "Take Wendy and the boys to the island! I'll stay here and draw the pirates' fire!"

Tinker Bell took off at once for Peter's hideaway. But she purposely flew too fast, leaving the others far behind.

"Tinker Bell! Wait for us! We can't keep up with you!" yelled Wendy and the boys.

But Tink didn't want to wait. Peter Pan had hardly looked at Tinker Bell since Wendy had come along. Tink didn't like it one bit, and now she had a plan!

Tinker Bell zoomed ahead, flying into an opening in a tree where the Lost Boys and Peter lived. Jingling in her pixie language, she told the boys Peter had sent her with a message that there was a terrible "Wendy-bird" headed their way. Peter's orders were to shoot it down!

The Lost Boys hurried out from their hiding place.

"I see it!" yelled Skunk as he and the others placed stones in their slingshots.

"Ready...aim...fire!" shouted the boys. Suddenly rocks were flying everywhere, hitting Wendy and sending her tumbling from the sky!

Luckily, Peter Pan arrived just in time to catch Wendy. "Peter...you saved my life," said Wendy, throwing her arms around him.

"I bring you a mother to tell you stories," Peter angrily told the Lost Boys, "and you shoot her down!"

"B-b-but Tink said it was a bird," stammered Cubby.

"She said you said to shoot it," added Rabbit.

"Tinker Bell," said Peter, "you might have killed Wendy!
I hereby banish you forever!"

"Please," begged Wendy, feeling sorry for poor Tinker Bell,
"not forever!"

"For a week, then!" declared Peter.

Taking Wendy by the hand, Peter flew off to show her Mermaid Lagoon. John and Michael wanted to explore Never Land, too, but had no interest in mermaids. They wanted to see Indians.

"John, you be the leader," declared the Lost Boys. Then, lining up behind him, they marched off into the forest.

As they marched along, the Lost Boys and John made a plan. They would be very clever and capture the Indians!

It might have worked, too, except for one thing—the Indians caught them first.

Michael and John were very frightened until the Lost Boys explained how things worked. "When we win, we turn them loose. When they win, they turn us loose."

But this time the Indian Chief wouldn't set the Lost Boys free. He thought that they had kidnapped his daughter, Tiger Lily.

"You tell me where you hid Princess Tiger Lily," the Chief said, "or you'll burn at the stake!"

45

Meanwhile, Peter was showing Wendy the
beautiful Mermaid Lagoon when he suddenly
spotted Hook and Smee rowing by in a small boat.
Tied up in back was Tiger Lily! "It looks like
they're headed for Skull Rock," Peter whispered
to Wendy. "Let's see what they're up to."

Sure enough, Hook was holding Tiger Lily prisoner in Skull Rock. "Tell me the hiding place of Peter Pan and I shall set you free. Hurry, before the tide comes in!" Hook demanded.

Peter was ready to rescue Tiger Lily. "I'll show the old codfish. Stay here, Wendy, and watch the fun!" Then he drew his dagger and challenged Hook to a fight.

Hook slashed at Peter! Peter jumped away just in time! Then Peter pinned the captain, but Hook broke free and fought Peter to the very edge of a cliff.

"I've got you this time, Pan!" he cried.

Peter backed away from Hook.

Hook followed. Aaaahhhh! He went tumbling off the cliff!
"I'll get you for this, Pan!" he yelled. Then, as he fell toward
the water, Hook heard a familiar sound...tick-tock, tick-tock,
tick-tock. The crocodile was waiting.

"I say, Hook," grinned Peter Pan, "do you hear something?"

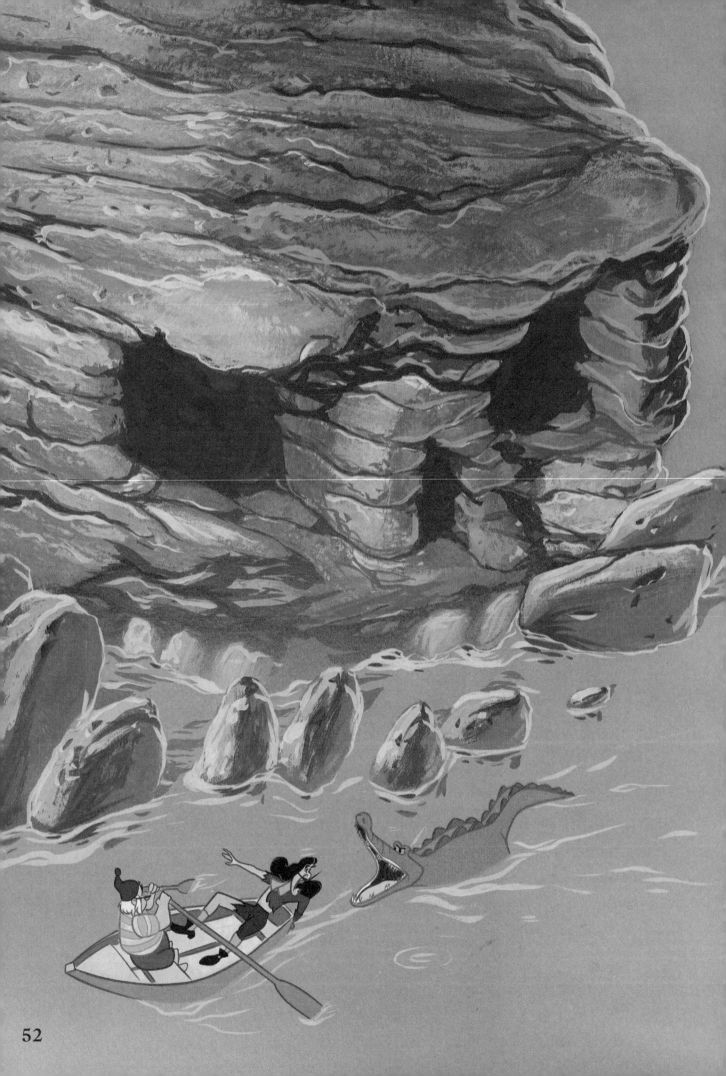

The crocodile swallowed the captain! But the terrified Hook fought furiously and jumped right back out!

"Smee! Smee!" Hook screamed as he tumbled into the boat. "Row for the ship! Row for the ship!"

While Smee rowed as fast as he could, Peter swooped down to save Tiger Lily and fly her back home.

The Indian Chief was so happy to see his daughter again
that he freed John, Michael, and the Lost Boys. Then he placed
a headdress of beautiful feathers on Peter Pan, proclaiming
Peter Pan "Chief Little Flying Eagle."

"Waaawhoop!" yelled Peter.

"Oh, how wonderful!" said Wendy.

"Bravo!" added John.

But there was someone who was not joining in the celebration. Poor Tinker Bell was all alone without Peter or her friends, the Lost Boys. And she wasn't happy at all.

And that's just how Smee found Tinker
Bell...all alone, sitting by herself.

"Beggin' your pardon, Miss Bell," said Smee,
catching Tinker Bell in his knit cap, "but Cap'n
Hook would like a word with you."

The Captain wanted a word, all right—several of them. "We sail in the morning," he told Tinker Bell. If she would only tell him where Peter's hideout was, why, he'd take Wendy to sea with him. "With her gone, Peter will soon forget this mad infatuation!"

Sick with jealousy and loneliness, Tinker Bell fell for Hook's evil plan and showed him how to find Peter's hideaway!

At Peter's hideaway, all was cozy and quiet. Wendy, acting as a good mother should, was tucking the boys into bed. As she did, she sang to them about the wonders of a real mother.

By the time Wendy had finished her song, John and Michael were so homesick that they wanted to leave for London at once. Even the Lost Boys wanted to go.

But not Peter. "Go back and grow up!" he said stubbornly. "But I'm warnin' you, once you're grown up, you can never come back!"

But no one was listening to Peter. They had only one thought on their minds: a mother to love them and hold them and sing them to sleep at night. One by one, the boys left Peter's hideaway—only to walk right into the arms of the waiting pirates!

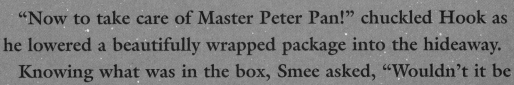

"Now to take care of Master Peter Pan!" chuckled Hook as he lowered a beautifully wrapped package into the hideaway.

Knowing what was in the box, Smee asked, "Wouldn't it be more human-like to slit his throat?"

"Aye," laughed Hook, "but I have given Tinker Bell me word not to lay a finger—or a hook—on Peter Pan. And Captain Hook never breaks a promise!"

Tying his prisoners to the mast of his pirate ship, Hook warned them, "Join us or walk the plank."

"Never," declared Wendy. "Peter Pan will save us."

"My dear," said Hook, "we left a present for Peter, a sort of surprise package. I can see our little friend at this very moment, reading the tender note, 'To Peter, with love, from Wendy.' Could he but see within the package, he would find an ingenious little device set so that when it is six o'clock he will be blasted out of Never Land forever!"

Hearing Hook's evil plan, a desperate Tinker Bell knocked over the lantern where Hook held her prisoner. Crack! went the glass. Tinker Bell was free! Off she flew to try to save Peter.

Back in his hideout, Peter Pan picked up the package and was just untying the bow when Tinker Bell flew in.

"Hi, Tink," said Peter, holding up the box. "Look what Wendy left."

Tinker Bell tried to pull the package away. "Stop that!" yelled Peter. "What's the matter with you?"

There was no time to explain. Tink flew at the box, pushing it as far from Peter as she could. The gift began to smoke. And then...kaboom!

The explosion was so huge, it rocked the pirate ship! Hook removed his hat and bowed. "And so passeth a worthy opponent!"

Smiling, Hook turned to the captive children.
"Which will it be? Join me crew or walk the plank!"

Wendy spoke up bravely. "Captain Hook, we will
never join your crew."

Hook gave Wendy his most gentlemanly bow.
"Ladies first, my dear!" With tears trickling down her
cheeks, Wendy walked the plank. One step, then
another, closer and closer to the edge, until
finally...she jumped!

Now it was the pirates' turn to quake with fear.
"Cap'n," said Smee, "there was no splash!"
"The ship's bewitched!" the men began to wail.
But it wasn't a ghost who had come to haunt
Hook. It was Peter, along with Tinker Bell, who
had escaped Hook's bomb. Now he had come to
save Wendy!

"This time you've gone too far!" shouted Peter Pan as he flew up onto the rigging. Hook scrambled up after him, then drew his sword.

"Take that!" cried Hook as he lunged at Peter, forcing him off balance. "I'll run you through!"

Peter quickly flew out of Hook's way, cutting this way and that with his dagger.

"You wouldn't dare fight old Hook man to man," taunted the Captain. "You'd fly away like a cowardly sparrow."

"I'll fight you man to man with one hand behind my back!" crowed Peter.

As Wendy, John, Michael, and the Lost Boys fought the pirate crew, Hook took a powerful swing at Peter. But the Captain lost his balance!

Down, down, down fell Captain Hook...to face his worst fear. The crocodile was waiting, and its mouth was wide open!

The last Peter, Wendy, John, Michael, or the Lost Boys heard of the terrible Captain Hook were his calls for help.

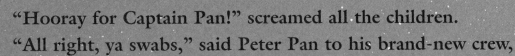

"Hooray for Captain Pan!" screamed all the children.

"All right, ya swabs," said Peter Pan to his brand-new crew, "we're castin' off!"

"But...but...Peter," stammered Wendy, "could you tell me, sir, where we're sailing?"

"To London, madam!" said Peter.

"Michael, John, we're going home!" Wendy smiled.

"Hoist the anchor!" cried Peter to his crew. "Tink, let's have some pixie dust!"

Tinker Bell flew all around the ship, sprinkling her magical dust as she went. Then up, up, up went the ship, and as it rose, it began to glow like gold.

"Wendy," said Mrs. Darling. She was gently shaking her daughter, whom she had found asleep by the window.

"Oh, Mother, we're back!" announced Wendy as she woke.

"Back?" asked Mr. Darling.

"All except the Lost Boys," explained Wendy. "They weren't quite ready to grow up. It was such a wonderful adventure! Tinker Bell and mermaids and Peter Pan. We sailed away in a ship in the sky...."

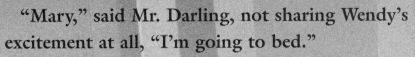

"Mary," said Mr. Darling, not sharing Wendy's excitement at all, "I'm going to bed."

But as he turned to leave, Mr. Darling paused to look up into the night sky. There, crossing in front of the moon, was a ship made of clouds. "You know," said Mr. Darling, "I have the strangest feeling I've seen that ship before. A long time ago, when I was very young."

And, indeed, he had.

Disney's Classic Storybook COLLECTION™

Relive the movies one book at a time.

ALADDIN
ALICE IN WONDERLAND
THE ARISTOCATS
BAMBI
BEAUTY AND THE BEAST

THE BLACK CAULDRON
CINDERELLA
DUMBO
THE FOX AND THE HOUND
THE GREAT MOUSE DETECTIVE

HERCULES
THE HUNCHBACK OF NOTRE DAME
THE JUNGLE BOOK
LADY AND THE TRAMP
THE LION KING

THE LITTLE MERMAID
MICKEY'S CHRISTMAS CAROL
OLIVER & COMPANY
ONE HUNDRED AND ONE DALMATIANS
PETER PAN

PINOCCHIO
POCAHONTAS
THE RESCUERS
THE RESCUERS DOWN UNDER
ROBIN HOOD

SLEEPING BEAUTY
SNOW WHITE AND THE SEVEN DWARFS
THE SWORD IN THE STONE
TOY STORY
WINNIE THE POOH

For you... from MOUSE WORKS

A special invitation to have even more fun—
Free!

Send for a FREE ISSUE of FamilyFun Magazine! It's chock full of fun activities the whole family will love!

⭐ Easy after-school and rainy-day activities. Like how to create a cloud – or make tin-can stilts!

⭐ Great crafts & hobbies with step-by-step instructions. Like how to splatter a T-shirt or make thrilling, chilling Halloween costumes!

⭐ Fun party plans, dynamite decorations, and great games. Like how to dance the hula in a paper grass skirt and make a lei out of pasta!

⭐ Recipes kids love to make – and eat! Imagine carrot "coins", broccoli "trees", and baked potatoes "a la Mode."

⭐ And everything else fun from family computing to family traveling to Family Olympics. Imagine tie-dying socks – or making "duck feet" to have a Duck Foot Relay Race!

You always know what you'll find in FamilyFun – 100% activities and 100% fun! And it's free with this special invitation!

Just send in the FREE ISSUE Certificate today!

FamilyFun
Free Issue Certificate

Yes! Send my family the next issue of FamilyFun – FREE! If we like it, we'll get a full year (10 big issues in all, including my free issue and TWO SPECIAL ISSUES) for just $11.95. We'll SAVE 54% off the cover price! If we choose not to subscribe, we'll return the bill marked "cancel", and owe nothing. The FREE issue is ours to keep.

Name _____ (please print)

Address _____

City/State/Zip _____

(Optional) gender of child/children (boy/girl) _____ Birthdate(s) _____

FamilyFun's newsstand price is $25.90 a year. In Canada, add $10 (U.S. funds) for postage and GST. Other foreign orders, add $20 (U.S. funds). First issue mails within 6-8 weeks. Offer valid through June 30, 2000. © Disney

Includes TWO SPECIAL ISSUES at no extra cost!

L7MW

FamilyFun

100% activities. 100% fun.

From Disney

"Your magazine is absolutely fantastic! It has everything I have been looking for in a magazine and have never been able to find."
— Peggy Bertsch, Sandusky, Ohio

"Fresh ideas for getting involved with my kids — isn't that what parenting is all about? Thank you, thank you, thank you."
— Cathy Zirkelbach, Denver, Colorado

"This is the best magazine for families I have ever seen. I will keep my issues forever."
— Carol A. Green, Lee's Summit, Missouri

"I have read FamilyFun front to back twice and have shared articles with almost everyone I know. Our family has tried recipes and activities — and we haven't had a flop yet! I only wish we had discovered you sooner."
— Mary Balcom, Rochester Hills, Michigan

FREE ISSUE!

FamilyFun
Great Island Towns!
Beach Vacations Families Love
HOST A COWBOY COOKOUT
You Can Hike with Kids
18 Top Family Dogs
Crafts for Beachcombers

Yours free!

See why families everywhere are having so much fun with FamilyFun! Send for your FREE ISSUE today. If card is missing, write to FamilyFun Magazine, PO Box 37031, Boone, IA 50037-2031.